Black Sea

COLCHIS

ymplegades

Bosphorus

Isle of Ares

Isle of Bebryces

ASIA MINOR

Mediterranean Sea

For Imogen – J.R.
For Lynne Hudson – J.C.

JASON *and the* GOLDEN FLEECE

James Riordan

Illustrated by Jason Cockcroft

FRANCES LINCOLN CHILDREN'S BOOKS

First published in Great Britain in 2003 by Frances Lincoln Children's Books,
4 Torriano Mews, Torriano Avenue, London NW5 2RZ
www.franceslincoln.com

Distributed in the USA by Publishers Group West

First paperback edition 2005

British Library Cataloguing in Publication Data
available on request

ISBN 1-84507-061-5 paperback

Set in Sabon

Printed in China

1 3 5 7 9 8 6 4 2

JAMES RIORDAN

was born and grew up in Portsmouth.
He has lectured at Portsmouth Polytechnic and the Universities of Bradford and Birmingham and is now Professor Emeritus at the University of Surrey, Honorary Professor at Stirling and Hong Kong Baptist Universities, and has been awarded an Honorary Doctorate from L'Université Stendhal in Grenoble.
He is the author of many children's books, among them collections of Siberian, Korean, Irish and Russian Gypsy folk tales.
Sweet Clarinet, his first children's novel, was nominated for the Whitbread Prize in 1998 and won the NASEN award in 1999, while his second novel, *The Prisoner*, received a Carnegie Award nomination in 2000.
His first book for Frances Lincoln was *The Coming of Night*, and was followed by *The Twelve Labours of Hercules*, which won the U.K. Reading Association Award 1998.

JASON COCKCROFT

was born in New Zealand and brought up in West Yorkshire, where he lives in Ilkley. He studied Illustration at Falmouth School of Art and began his career while still at art school, illustrating Helen Cresswell's *Sophie and the Seawolf* (Hodder).
He has illustrated books for authors including Leon Garfield, Michael Morpurgo, Jana Novotny Hunter, Maggie Pearson, Elizabeth Laird, Sally Grindley and Pippa Goodhart. His illustrations for Geraldine McCaughrean's retelling of *A Pilgrim's Progress* (Hodder) won the Blue Peter Children's Book Award in 2000. He has also illustrated the covers for the Harry Potter novels. *The Horse Girl*, written by Miriam Moss, was his first book for Frances Lincoln.

River Danube

GREECE

Salmydessos

THRACE

ITALY

Sea
Marma

Kyzikos

Hellespont

Mount Pelion

Iolcos

Lemnos

CRETE

ROUTE TAKEN BY THE *ARGO* FROM IOLCOS TO COLCHIS

Contents

Introduction 9
The Golden Fleece 10
The Centaur Chiron 13
Crossing the Stream 16
The Man with One Sandal 19
Launching the *Argo* 22
The Women of Lemnos 25
Bear Island 28
Hylas and the Water Nymphs 31
The Boxing Match 34
Blind Phineus and the Harpies 37
The Clashing Rocks 39
Medea 42
The Impossible Tasks 45
Capturing the Fleece 48
The Pursuit 50
Poseidon's Wrath 53
Return of the *Argo* 55
The Death of Jason 58
Sources 61

Introduction

Jason's quest for the mysterious Golden Fleece is one of the oldest of Greek legends. Homer, writing in the 7th century B.C., referred to the story in his Iliad and Odyssey as if his readers already knew it well. Throughout the ancient world, the voyage of Jason and the Argonauts from Greece to Colchis in the Black Sea inspired song and verse, painting and sculpture.

Although Jason is mentioned only in passing by Homer, Hesiod and the Theban poet Pindar, he features more prominently with his wife Medea in Euripedes' tragedy Medea, written in 431 B.C. But it is the Argonautika, a play written by the Rhodes scholar Apollonius in the 3rd century B.C., that gives the first full account of Jason's voyage. While Pindar and Euripedes portray Medea as the villain of the piece and the cause of Jason's downfall, Apollonius tells a different tale. Instead of making Medea a scheming witch, he depicts her as a victim of Jason's determination to win the Golden Fleece.

Whatever his failings, Jason was a great hero – the first in a distinguished line of Greek heroes that was to include Herakles (who is called Hercules in this book because that is the name most people know him by) and Odysseus. Through the ages, many a Greek family has claimed blood ties with the Argonauts, and Jason has served as a model for all daring seafarers, from Christopher Columbus to Drake and Thor Heyerdahl. He is a supreme example of courage and adventure, a man who overcame all dangers to reach his goal.

The Golden Fleece

"Sacrifice your children to Zeus! Then the corn will grow." Thus spoke the Oracle of Delphi to Athemas, King of Thebes.

It was a cruel price to pay for corn. But the king knew that without bread the Thebans would starve. Fire had destroyed their stores of grain, and now, unless a harvest grew from the withered seeds, famine would destroy the land.

Tearfully, the king agreed that his beloved children should die. Little did he realise that Ino, his new queen, had bribed the Oracle to deceive him. She wanted her stepchildren dead, so that her own son could inherit the throne.

So it was, at noon on the fateful day, that white-robed priests solemnly led the two children to the hilltop altar where they were to die.

Then a strange thing happened. All at once, a thunderbolt exploded in the sky above them, and Zeus, father of the gods, glared down in anger. "I will not permit this crime!" he roared. His rage thundered through the hills, his fury flashed across the plain.

As the priests drew back in fear, down from the sky flew two figures: Hermes, silver-winged messenger of the gods, and Aries, their sacred ram. The ram's golden fleece gleamed so brightly in the midday sun that everyone had to shield their eyes.

"Climb up on the ram!" cried Hermes to the children.

The priests stood transfixed as Phrixus and his sister Helle mounted the ram's broad back and clung fast to its thick wool. Then up they flew, up, up into the clouds and out over the sea; on and on above the blue Aegean until they reached the narrow strait where Europe and Asia meet.

Just then, little Helle, who was numb with cold, lost her grip. She plunged down into the sea and drowned. Ever since, people have called those straits the Hellespont – Helle's Sea.

Aries, Hermes and Phrixus flew on, eastwards over dark brooding waters until they reached Colchis on the Black Sea shore, where the white-topped mountains of the Caucasus rise higher than the sky. Hermes pointed to a splendid palace spread out below, and they flew down towards it.

They alighted in the palace courtyard where Aetes, king of that region, was taking his ease.

"Don't be alarmed," said Hermes to the startled king. Then he told him what had happened, adding, "If you grant this young prince protection, you may keep the Golden Fleece."

Eyeing the Fleece gleaming in the sunlight, Aetes eagerly agreed. So the king's men sheared the Fleece from the ram's back, and Hermes and Aries flew off to Greece, leaving Prince Phrixus in Aetes' care.

But King Aetes had no intention of harbouring a foreign prince who might one day claim the Fleece. Now that he had his glittering prize, he had no further use for Phrixus.

"Put the boy to death!" he commanded.

As for the Fleece, fearful that the Greeks might come to take it back, Aetes hung it high in an olive grove beyond the palace walls. There it cast a glow like the setting sun over the countryside around. To guard the Fleece, he put a hissing serpent in the grove, which wound its thick coils about the tree. Its scaly head swayed to and fro, one eye open all the time – even when it slept.

"No one can steal my treasure now," thought the king.

But he was wrong. Far across the seas a youth was growing to manhood. One day, he would avenge Phrixus' cruel death, rescue the Golden Fleece and bring it home to Greece.

The CENTAUR CHIRON

In a cave high on the rocky slopes of Mount Pelion, overlooking the port of Iolcos, lived Chiron, oldest and wisest of the centaurs. This white-bearded half-man, half-horse was held in such high esteem that many a Greek family entrusted its sons' education to him.

Chiron taught his pupils hunting and fighting skills, as well as music, poetry and mathematics. He even instructed them in healing the sick and reading the stars. Amid the rugged peaks, Chiron's charges learned to brave the winter snows and summer sun wearing only the hides of animals slain with weapons they themselves had made.

Among Chiron's pupils were boys who later became heroes – Hercules, Aeneas and Achilles. But Jason was to be the bravest of them all. By the time he reached manhood, he was a tall, bronzed youth with flowing fair hair and grey-green eyes. His dress was a leopard skin won with a spear cut from mountain ash.

One day, Chiron summoned the youth and they sat together at the mouth of a cave overlooking the shimmering sea.

"Long ago," began the centaur, "this kingdom was ruled by a noble king called Aeson – until one day his wicked brother Pelias stole his throne and killed his brother's children. So when Aeson's wife Polymele had another son, to save his life she entrusted him to my care."

He paused, and looked keenly at Jason before continuing, "That was twenty years ago. Now it is time for that prince to reclaim his crown."

At once Jason saw the meaning of Chiron's words. He was King Aeson's son! The rich city, green plain and busy port on which he had so often gazed from the cloud-wrapped peaks were all his heritage.

"Go now," said Chiron, "and remember what I have taught you. Heed this too: the gods intend you for great deeds. One day, Greeks will revere your name, for you will be the greatest hero of them all."

With Chiron's words echoing in his ears, Jason bade farewell to his tutor and friends and set off for the plain below.

Crossing *the* Stream

Under a bright morning sun, Jason bounded down the rocky slopes. Soon he reached the cool shade of pines growing in the foothills, and thrust his way through the tangled vine. By mid-afternoon he stood before an open plain: stretching ahead were fields of corn, lush green meadows and groves of lemon trees. But to reach them, he had to cross a river swollen by melting snows.

He was about to plunge into the icy water when he spotted an old woman squatting on the bank. She was dressed in tattered rags and rocked to and fro as she stared into the swollen stream. Seeing Jason, she cried out in a feeble voice, "Help me! Help me ford the stream!"

Glancing from the old woman to the torrent, Jason hesitated. But mindful of Chiron's words, he said with a sigh, "My shoulders are broad enough for such a skinny load as you. Up, mother! I will gladly carry you across."

Bending down, he took the woman on his back, leapt into the foam and struggled through the swell. Yet so heavy was she, and so tightly did her fingers clutch his neck, that it took all his strength to reach the distant shore. And all the while, the old woman grumbled, "You're wetting my clothes! You're trying to drown me!"

She was so ungrateful, Jason felt like tossing her from his back. But patiently he soothed her with gentle words, and battled on until he reached the bank. Once he had set her down, he bent to secure his sandal – for he had lost the other in the muddy river-bed and cut his bare foot on a stone.

When he looked up, he was amazed to see a tall, stately woman dressed in dazzling white. Her smiling eyes shone with such a radiant light, he knew at once she was divine.

"Never mind your missing sandal, Jason," she said. "Its loss will be your gain. I am Hera, mother of the gods and I came to put you to the test. Since you bent your back to help a needy soul, my Oracle will always aid you in your hour of need. Go now to Iolcos and face the king."

Jason fell to his knees, thankful he had been true to Chiron's teaching. When he looked up, Hera had gone. So he went on his way limping, with only one sandal, wondering what fate awaited him at the court of Pelias.

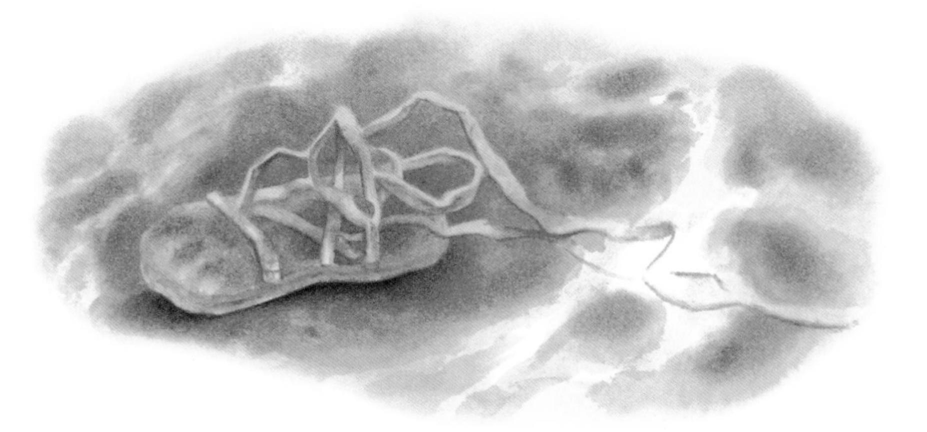

The Man *with* One Sandal

As evening cast its shadows on the road, Jason passed through the wooden gates and entered the city of his birth. There, to his surprise, he found himself the centre of attention. Not only were people stopping to admire the bold, bronzed youth, they were staring and pointing at his foot.

"The man with one sandal!" they kept whispering.

When Jason asked what they meant, a woman explained, "The Oracle has foretold that when a stranger in a single sandal comes, he will depose the king." Then Jason recalled Hera's words: *Its loss will be your gain.*

He made his way to the palace and asked to see the king. When at last he entered the hall, he noticed Pelias' gaze straying to his foot. The king was clearly ill at ease, especially when Jason announced, "King Pelias, I have come to claim the throne that is my birthright."

All the same, Pelias pretended to welcome his long-lost nephew.

"Your claim may well be just," he replied. "By all means, take the crown – if you can prove yourself a worthy king. But how can we be sure you are fit to rule? What brave deeds have you performed?"

Jason confessed, "None so far, but I'll take on anything you say."

The crafty monarch rubbed his chin and asked, "Would you fetch the Golden Fleece?"

Now, sitting round Chiron's fire at night, Jason had often heard the tale of Prince Phrixus and Princess Helle, of their flight across the seas, the gift of the Golden Fleece, and how the king had murdered the prince. It was a tale to stir any hero's heart, and many dreamed of making the quest to bring back the Fleece. Yet none had been rash enough to try.

"If I were younger," said the king, for all to hear, "I would go myself. Where can I find a hero to bring the Fleece back home to Greece?"

There and then, Jason made up his mind.

"I'll do it!" he cried.

Launching *the* Argo

King Pelias was sure that Jason's quest would fail. No ship had ever braved such unknown seas. So he gave Jason ample funds, hoping to rid himself of the young pretender to his throne.

First of all, Jason went secretly to Hera's sacred grove at Dodona, in north-west Greece. There he prayed to her Oracle – a talking oak – which, as she had promised, told him what to do.

"Hire the boat-builder Argos of Thespia," the Oracle said. "Athene, goddess-guardian of heroes, will guide his hand. Tell him to make the hull and fifty oars from Mount Pelion's seasoned pine. Then sew sails of strong white cloth. For the prow, take a branch of this sacred oak and carve a figurehead. Whenever you're in danger, it will tell you what to do."

So Jason hired Argos to build the ship.

Meanwhile, he set about assembling his crew. From every corner of the land, the bold, the brave and the strong thronged to Iolcos' shores. Mighty Hercules came, fresh from his first labours at Mycenae, with his young friend Hylas; the twins Castor and Pollux from Sparta, famed for their fighting skills; Theseus from Athens, destined one day to slay the Minotaur; the warrior Nestor, who would later fight at Troy; Orpheus, bard of Thrace, son of the god Apollo; Argos the ship-builder; sharp-eyed Lynceus, who was to be the ship's pilot;

Tiphys the Boeotian helmsman. Even Acastus, son of King Pelias, came – he stole away to enlist, against his father's will. And one woman joined the band. She was Atalanta of Arcadia, the greatest huntress in Greece. Atalanta could outrun any male and match the best of them with her bow. There were fifty crew in all.

When the ship was finished, it was the biggest, strongest vessel ever seen. So light was it, the crew could carry it on their shoulders. Yet it was strong enough to brave the stormiest seas. Jason named it the *Argo*, after its creator, and called his crew 'the Argonauts'.

After settling the fifty seats by lot, Jason prepared to launch the ship. The Argonauts untied the laurel cord and hauled up the anchor-stone. Then they bent their backs to row clear of the treacherous rocks and sandbanks near the harbour mouth.

Once out in the Aegean, they hoisted high the lofty mast and vast white sails. A fair wind swelled the cloth and the great vessel braved the open sea. Meanwhile, high in the stern, Orpheus sang so sweetly to his lyre that the Argonauts' hearts soared at the sound.

So, guided by the stars, the heroes began their long voyage to the misty shores of Colchis, at the other end of the world.

The WOMEN *of* LEMNOS

At first, a gentle breeze bore the ship along. But after a while the zephyr gave way to gusts of wailing wind which stirred up angry seas. Amid towering waves and clashing foam, one or too faint hearts among the crew feared their end had come – almost before the voyage had begun.

Then, all at once, a rocky island loomed in sight, dipping and rising with the swell. Glad to find a haven from the storm, the Argonauts rowed with all their might toward the bay. As they drew near, odd snatches of song drifted on the breeze, a song so magical it drew them past the jagged rocks and safely into shore.

Inside the harbour, the wind died to a breathless calm and the crew saw a crowd of women waiting on the strand. They were holding out their arms in welcome and raising sweet voices in happy song. There was not a man to be seen.

The heroes found themselves surrounded by eager women, several to a man. It was not long before they yielded to the women's charms. As for Jason, the queen of that island, whose name was Hypsipyle, invited him to share her throne. Only Atalanta and Hercules stayed with the ship, both impatient to sail on.

So sweet was love, so mild the mood, so tender the caress, that the men lingered on and on. They lost all desire to leave. As the months passed, many homes rang to the sound of infant cries; and Jason fathered twin sons with Hypsipyle.

The queen told Jason the islanders' tale: "Lemnos was once a joyful place filled with laughter and family love. But one day, a young Lemnian girl gazed at her reflection in a pool – at her olive skin, dark eyes and silken hair – and sang that surely none was prettier than she. Jealous Aphrodite heard her boast and flew into a rage. How dare a mortal claim to be more beautiful than the goddess of love! And she punished all the Lemnian women. Such cruel revenge: so badly did she make us smell that our menfolk left and found new wives in Thrace.

"When the men returned with Thracian wives, we were so angry that we drove away the women and killed every male, young and old alike. Too late, Aphrodite removed the curse. For not a single man remained to father children. Now you have come, and we can bear children again."

Listening to this tale, Jason was afraid the women might one day treat his crew as they had their own men. Yet so deeply were the Argonauts under the women's spell that none would agree to leave.

In the end, Hercules changed their minds. He lost patience and strode through the town, beating on doors and reminding the heroes of their quest. Reluctantly, the men made their farewells and left that very night, exchanging warm kisses for the chill spray of the sea. On they sailed, fearful of the dangers that lay ahead; but no one suspected the twist of fate that was to come.

Bear Island

Jason set sail for the Hellespont, that narrow neck of sea below which Helle's bones lay resting on the sand. The *Argo* waited until nightfall before slipping with muffled oars through the channel guarded by King Laomedon of Troy.

Dawn found the Argonauts safe in the Sea of Marmara, the Marble Sea, sailing up the Dolonian coast. Since they needed fresh food and water, they headed for a friendly port where they might land. At Arcton, on Bear Island, they were in luck, for young King Kyzikos had just wed the lovely Kleite of Phrygia, and he invited the heroes to his wedding feast.

Once again Hercules remained on board, this time with three other men to guard the ship. It was fortunate they did. While the king and his guests were feasting, out of the hills rushed a savage horde of six-armed giants – bear-like beasts covered in thick black fur. They were hurling rocks from every hand. But Hercules and his men fired their arrows so swiftly into the attacking horde that soon none remained alive.

Next day, it was a happy king and queen who bade the heroes farewell, grateful to them for ridding the island of the giant bears.

As the *Argo* headed for the Bosphorus, however, a fierce north-easterly breeze blew up, whirling the ship about. It finally

came to shelter in the lee of an unfamiliar shore. The winds were high, the rain lashed down and the tide rolled darkly up the sand as the heroes beached their ship.

The shadows of night enveloped them in a veil. And in the gloom, a band of well-armed warriors came swooping down to attack them. But they were no match for the Argonauts, who fought them off and left many dead upon the strand.

Only as morning broke did they discover the terrible truth. They had landed back at Bear Island and slain the very men with whom they had feasted the night before! The islanders had mistaken them for pirates! King Kyzikos lay dead, slain by Jason's sword.

When Kleite, the king's widowed bride, heard the news, she hanged herself in grief. As for the Argonauts, remorse filled their hearts and for three long days they held funeral games to honour the dead. It was a sombre crew that left those sad shores.

Hylas *and the* Water Nymphs

Dark clouds above and silent tides below matched the melancholy mood. The rowers bent double over their oars as they made slow headway through the Marble Sea.

It was mighty Hercules who hit on a plan to lift the spirits of the crew. "Let's have a contest," he cried. "See who can outrow the rest!" He thought that aching muscles might dispel their gloom.

With Tiphys at the helm and Orpheus at the lyre, the heroes arched their backs and plied their oars. Muscles glistened, temples throbbed, throats groaned as they took the strain. And one by one the rowers wearily fell back. At last, only four remained: Jason and Hercules, Castor and Pollux.

Then the twins collapsed as one, leaving Jason and Hercules to duel on. Their brawny arms drove the ship through stubborn waves and up the Mysian coast until, eventually, Jason fainted with fatigue. But at the same moment, Hercules' oar broke with a mighty crack and he tumbled off his seat. Red-faced, he glared about, daring anyone to laugh – or he'd lay his broken oar across their back!

Spirits raised, the crew put ashore. While others went to fill their gourds, Hercules set about cutting another oar. He soon found a sturdy pine, pulled it up by the roots and stripped it down.

"Hylas, come and lend a hand!" he yelled to his young friend. But the lad was nowhere to be seen.

Now, Hylas was the darling of the crew, a boy of tender years. His graceful limbs and pretty face would have sent jealous Aphrodite wild. When a search party went out to look for him, they found his bronze urn beside a spring – but of Hylas there was no sign. Hercules hunted high and low, and vowed not to leave until he'd found the boy.

At dawn next day, an anxious Jason stood waiting on the shore: Hercules had still not returned. And when a favourable breeze sprang up, Jason decided to consult Hera's prow. "What shall I do?" he asked.

"Catch the tide," replied the Oracle, "with or without Hercules."

So they hauled up the anchor stone, wondering about the fate of Hercules and Hylas. Then an unexpected event allayed their fears. For as the *Argo* put to sea, a green-bearded figure rose from the waves. It was Glaucus, the herald of sea-god Poseidon. Swimming in front of the prow, he cried, "Fear not! Hercules has gone to Mycenae to complete his labours. As for Hylas, he has found another destiny. When Dryope and her sister nymphs saw him drawing water at their lily-mantled pool, they were bewitched by his beauty. They put their arms about him and lured him with love to their underwater home, where he is now living happily."

Glaucus had set their minds at rest. They thanked him and sailed on. Although they missed the strength of Hercules at the oar and the gay company of Hylas, other matters soon occupied their minds.

The Boxing Match

A new hazard awaited them at the port of Bebryces. King Amycus of Bebryces was a son of Poseidon, a burly black-bearded, black-hearted giant of a man. It was his custom to stop passing ships and offer their crews a grim choice: either they put up a champion for a boxing match with him – or they would be hurled from the clifftop into the sea. No one had ever defeated the tyrant.

When Amycus threw down his challenge to the Argonauts, Pollux volunteered to take on the king. He had fought at the Olympic Games and won all his bouts. All the same, it was an uneven match. Not only was the king a head taller, but while Pollux was strapping his fists with leather thongs, Amycus fitted spiked bands on his own hands – one blow would fell an ox.

The Argonauts and Bebrycans lined up on opposite sides of a grassy space to cheer on their champions.

Pollux was unafraid. He danced nimbly round, letting Amycus tire himself out with bull-like rushes and wild swings. Now and then, when the king dropped his guard, Pollux pummelled his midriff and gaping mouth. But the hero himself did not go unharmed, for the king's supporters tripped him up and spun him round.

By the time the sun was sinking in the western sky, both men were running blood and desperately tired. It was then that Pollux turned

the king into the blinding sun; swiftly he landed a blow on the king's temple that knocked him out.

The king lay senseless. Pollux had triumphed.

As the Argonauts cheered their champion, the Bebrycans let out howls of rage, snatched up their swords and rushed at Pollux and his friends. But the Greeks were ready for them, and they dealt with the charging mob as Pollux had with their king.

When the fight was over, Jason once more consulted Hera's Oracle. This time, she said to him, "Poseidon will be angry at his son's disgrace. Sacrifice twenty of the king's best bulls. That will set his mind at rest."

Once the sacrifice was made, the Argonauts put to sea with a strong breath billowing their sails. It seemed they had placated Poseidon, and he was helping them on their way to Salmydessos, on the Thracian coast.

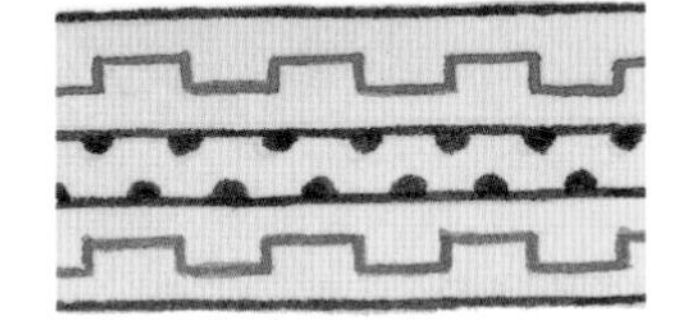

Blind Phineus *and the* Harpies

There was once a king who could foresee what was to come: Phineus was his name, and Salmydessos was his realm. But he angered the gods by predicting events they did not wish mortals to know. As a punishment they put out his eyes and sent three Harpies – winged monsters with hag-like heads and sharp eagle claws – to torment him.

Each time blind Phineus sat down to eat, the Harpies pounced upon his food and snatched it from his plate. He was forced to survive on the filthy scraps left by the vile creatures.

When the *Argo* put into the harbour at Salmydessos, King Phineus begged Jason's help. "Rid me of the Harpies," he said, "and I'll aid you with your quest." Now, Jason had heard of Phineus' oracular powers, so he readily agreed to help the king.

When the Argonauts were gathered around the king's table, servants brought in a splendid feast. And, as always, down swooped the Harpies, screeching and flapping their wings. This time, however, they met their match. Two of the heroes, Calais and Zetes, winged sons of Boreas, the north wind, sprang up, swords in hand. They chased the Harpies up into the sky and far across the sea, finally catching up with them above the Strophades Islands. And they would have slain the loathsome birds had not Iris, goddess of the rainbow, intervened.

She banished the Harpies to a dark cave in Crete, and they never troubled Phineus again.

So grateful was the king that he told the Argonauts about many events which were still to come. Yet, when questioned about the Golden Fleece, he was strangely silent.

"My son," he told Jason, "I cannot speak of the future lest I cross the gods again. All I will say is this: trust only in Hera, and in no other woman!"

The Clashing Rocks

With Phineus' words ringing in their ears, the Argonauts set sail for the mouth of the Black Sea. Easier said than done – for the *Argo* now had to sail through the Bosphorus, a narrow strait between two rocks known as the Symplegades. No vessel had ever passed through the strait. For when a ship tried to slip between the rocks, they would come together like clashing cymbals and grind it like grist in a mill.

But thanks to Phineus, the Argonauts knew what to do. The moment the heaving crags came in view, Jason released a white dove towards their gaping jaws. As soon as they sensed the bird, the dark rocks closed together with a snap! Too late: the dove slipped through with only a feather clipped before the rocks slowly opened again.

Now was the *Argo's* chance.

"Row for your lives!" yelled Jason. The heroes strained every sinew at the oar, pulling the blades so hard that the ship sprang forward like an arrow from a bow – straight between the rocks. The *Argo* bucked and leapt in the churning foam. And just as the steep crags loomed close on either side, the ship swept to safety on a huge wave. It was a close shave: the snapping jaws just grazed the stern.

The heroes rested on their oars, looking back with relief. Then a strange thing happened. With a noise like a thunderclap, the rocks of the Symplegades split apart and sank into the sea. Never again would they stop ships passing through the straits, thanks to the courage of the Argonauts.

But their delight was shortlived. For as the *Argo* was sailing up the southern shore, passing the isle of Ares, a great black cloud obscured the sun and it began to rain. But these were no ordinary raindrops: they were birds, terrible birds – the very creatures Hercules had once driven out of the Stymphalian Marsh. These monsters had wings, beaks and claws of brass and, whenever victims came in sight, they dropped showers of deadly darts.

Luckily, Phineus had forewarned the crew, and the Argonauts were ready. As the birds appeared, they locked shields above their heads and, when the rattling of darts had ceased, they banged their spears against the shields and scared the birds away. So they escaped unharmed.

Jason's crew braved many other dangers before they reached Colchis; some were fated never to see those shores. But after years at sea, those who remained finally sighted the menacing snow-topped peaks towering high above the shore. At long last they were nearing their goal.

Medea

On the day Jason strode into King Aetes' palace, he faced the hardest test of all. For the king had no intention of giving up the Golden Fleece.

Now, old Aetes owned two prized possessions: a set of magical dragon's teeth, and a pair of fire-breathing bulls. So when Jason announced his claim, the king thought for a moment, then declared, "In order to win the Fleece, you must do two things. First, you must yoke and harness my wild bulls to an iron plough and till a stony field. Second, you must sow the furrows with dragon's teeth – all between the rising and setting of the sun!"

The king smiled to himself. He knew such tasks were beyond any man.

But he reckoned without his daughter, Medea. As the young girl stood behind the throne, she stole shy glances at Jason. Eros had struck her heart with his arrow. Her cheeks were flushed, her heart beat wildly, her body was filled with newfound joy.

She watched closely as Jason spoke, the way he stood proudly before her father, how bold and fearless he looked. She had never seen a finer man.

Medea was only sixteen, as beautiful as the night wrapped in a thousand stars. And she was as mysterious as she was beautiful, for she was priestess to Hecate, goddess of witchcraft, and ministered at Hecate's temple with her handmaidens.

When Jason left the palace, his words still echoed in her ears, his face haunted her mind. "May he cheat death and return home safely," she said under her breath. But all the same, she was filled with foreboding.

She followed him, as fleeting as a shadow, her features darkly veiled. Once beyond the city walls, she drew aside her veil and shyly touched his sleeve. Turning, he recognised the pale daughter of his foe. Moonlight shone in her tender face and burnished her dark hair.

Now, Jason had heard of Medea's skills and he wondered how he might profit by them.

"Princess Medea," he began, "you are as wise as you are lovely. If you will help me, I shall be forever in your debt."

As he looked at her, her heart leapt in her breast.

"There might be a way," she said. "I can give you a special balm from the mountain crocus nourished on the blood of poor Prometheus.

It will protect you from my father's fire-breathing bulls. Go at midnight to Hecate's temple and cast off your clothes. Rub the balm over your body, then sprinkle drops upon your sword, spear and shield.

"One more thing. Tomorrow, when giants spring from the furrows you plough, toss a rock among them, then stand aside and let fate take its course."

Tears rolled down her cheeks. She knew he would soon be gone.

"Do not weep, princess," said Jason. "For what you have told me, the sons of Hellas will forever honour your name. As for me, I shall love you until my dying day."

At these words, such joy filled Medea's heart that she could not speak. They parted, and Jason hurried back to his crew.

On the stroke of midnight, he stood in Hecate's temple, oiling his body and weapons exactly as Medea had said. Gradually he felt a fearless power begin to course through his veins. He jumped for joy, rejoicing in his newfound strength and brandishing his ash spear, shield and sword of steel.

The Impossible Tasks

Next day at sunrise, a great crowd had gathered on the plain, waiting to see Jason perform his tasks. No one expected him to survive.

As King Aetes and the crowd drew back, Jason strode over to the stony field where the bronze yoke and iron plough stood ready to harness the mighty bulls. Their bellowing could be heard from a nearby cavern.

To everyone's surprise, Jason threw down his sword and spear into the soil and placed his helmet on the top. Then he stepped forward, stripped to the waist, bearing only a shield.

Out thundered the roaring bulls, their nostrils belching fire, their bronze feet clattering on the stony soil. Jason did not flinch. Catching one bull by the horns, he flung it on its back; then he wrestled the other to its knees. When both bulls were too tired to struggle further, he forced the yoke upon their humped necks and harnessed them to the plough. Though they still bellowed and raged like Furies, it did no good. All morning, Jason ploughed the field until deep, straight lines furrowed the rock-hard ground. By noon, his first task was done.

When the weary beasts were back in their cavern, the king, white-faced with anger, handed Jason a helmet filled with dragon's teeth as sharp as serpent fangs. And now, beneath the midday sun, Jason sowed the teeth in the fresh, upturned soil.

Strange seed it was! Instantly, the field began to stir and swell as if alive. The barren earth burst open and an army of giant men appeared, rising up from the soil with two-handled spears, stout shields and gleaming helmets.

As they advanced towards him, Medea's counsel served Jason well. He hurled a great rock into their midst and, at the sound, each warrior spun round like an eager hound.

"Who threw that rock?"

Then, as Jason leaned on his spear to watch, the men turned on one another, roaring for revenge; they fought so fiercely that soon the entire host lay dead, slain by each other's sword. By sunset the soil had swallowed up their flesh and feather grass covered their bones.

Jason had passed both tests!

The Argonauts and watching crowd let out a loud cheer. But the thwarted king could barely contain his rage.

"Tomorrow you'll have your reward," he said through gritted teeth. Already he was planning to burn the *Argo* and murder its crew before next dawn's light.

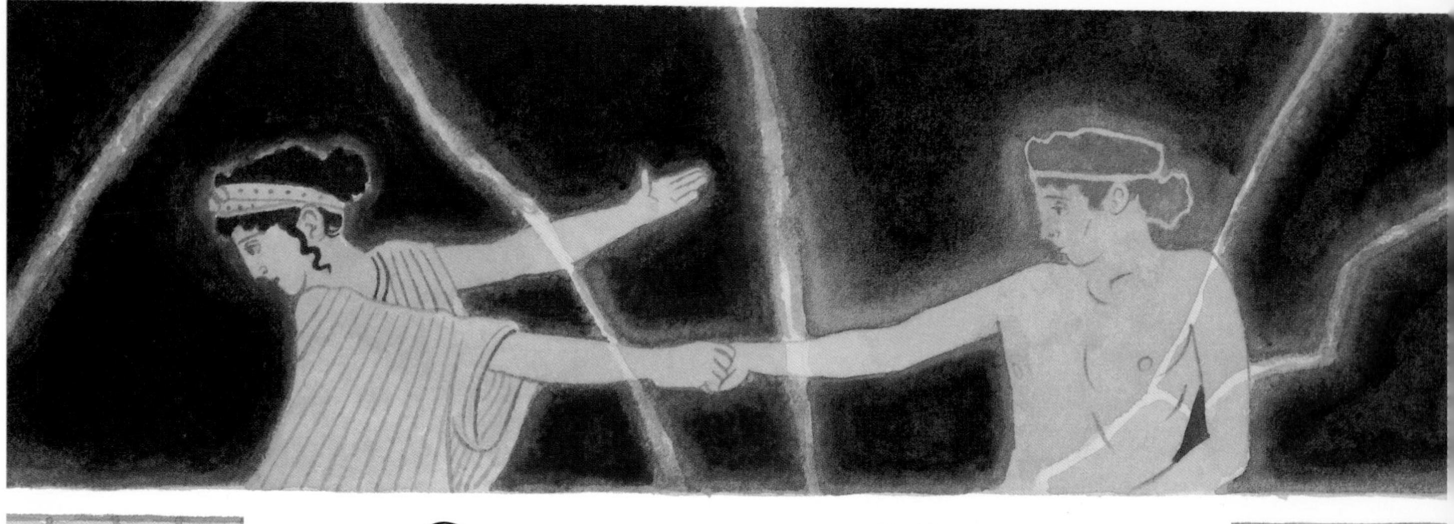

Capturing *the* Fleece

That night, Medea, fearing her father's wrath, said a tearful goodbye to her home and hurried down to the sea. There she called through the darkness. When Jason sprang ashore, she knelt down and flung her arms about his knees.

"Take me with you!" she begged. "I'll help you win the Golden Fleece, if only you will save me from my father."

Jason lifted her into his arms.

"As Hera is my witness," he said, "I'll make you my wife if you help me win the Golden Fleece." And he took her right hand in his, as a marriage vow.

So Medea led him to the sacred grove and pointed to where the Fleece was hanging, high in an olive tree. It gleamed like a mirror caught in the rays of the sun, shedding its golden glow throughout the grove.

Yet, even as they tiptoed through the grass, two glittering eyes were watching their every step. As they neared the base of the tree, the serpent reared up and opened its venomous jaws.

Jason would have drawn his sword, but Medea stayed his hand. Uttering a low chant, she stole forward and, as the scaly head swayed and hissed, she swiftly sprinkled its eyelids with a sleeping potion. The reptile grew drowsy. Its body slowly uncoiled from the tree and slipped to the ground. Soon it lay fast asleep.

This was Jason's chance. He stepped over the thick coils, clambered up the tree and seized the Golden Fleece.

"Be quick!" cried Medea. "We must hurry, before my father finds out."

Together they ran to the river mouth, where the Argonauts were waiting at their oars. The sun was almost up. When Jason held the Fleece aloft, their joyful shouts must have woken all Colchis!

Everyone wanted to touch the Fleece. But Jason spread it in the stern and seated Medea upon it.

"No more delay, my friends," he cried. "Hoist the sail for home! Thanks to Medea, we have our prize. She is coming with us – as my wife."

The PURSUIT

When King Aetes discovered that both his daughter and the Golden Fleece were gone, he was beside himself with rage. He commanded a fleet to be launched, and soon his ships covered the sea like crests on storm-tossed waves.

The Argonauts watched the pursuing ships with alarm. How they missed the strong arms of Hercules! Then Jason reminded them of Phineus' words: their return would take a course unknown to them.

"Phineus said that Hera would give us a sign," he said. And even as he spoke, the goddess did indeed send a portent. A shooting star suddenly blazed a trail far above them and disappeared over the horizon.

"That is where our passage lies!" cried Jason.

They set course by the mountains of Paphlagonia. But instead of rounding Cape Karambis and hugging the southern shore, they crossed the Black Sea to the Istros estuary.

As for the Colchians, blinded by mist, they sailed straight past Cape Karambis in pursuit.

But seeing no ships ahead, King Aetes guessed Jason's plan and sent his son Apsyrtos with a fleet of ships after the Argonauts. In his swift vessels, Apsyrtos made good time and took a short cut up Fair Mouth to the south of the estuary, intending to ambush the Argonauts upstream.

And Jason sailed right into Apsyrtos' trap.

What were the Argonauts to do now? Jason had no choice. They would have to trade Medea and the Golden Fleece to get home safely.

When she heard of Jason's plan, Medea was appalled. Angrily, she said, "Where are your honeyed promises? For you I gave up my home, my parents, all that I hold dear. It was thanks to me that you survived the bulls and the giants, and won the Golden Fleece. I am your wife!

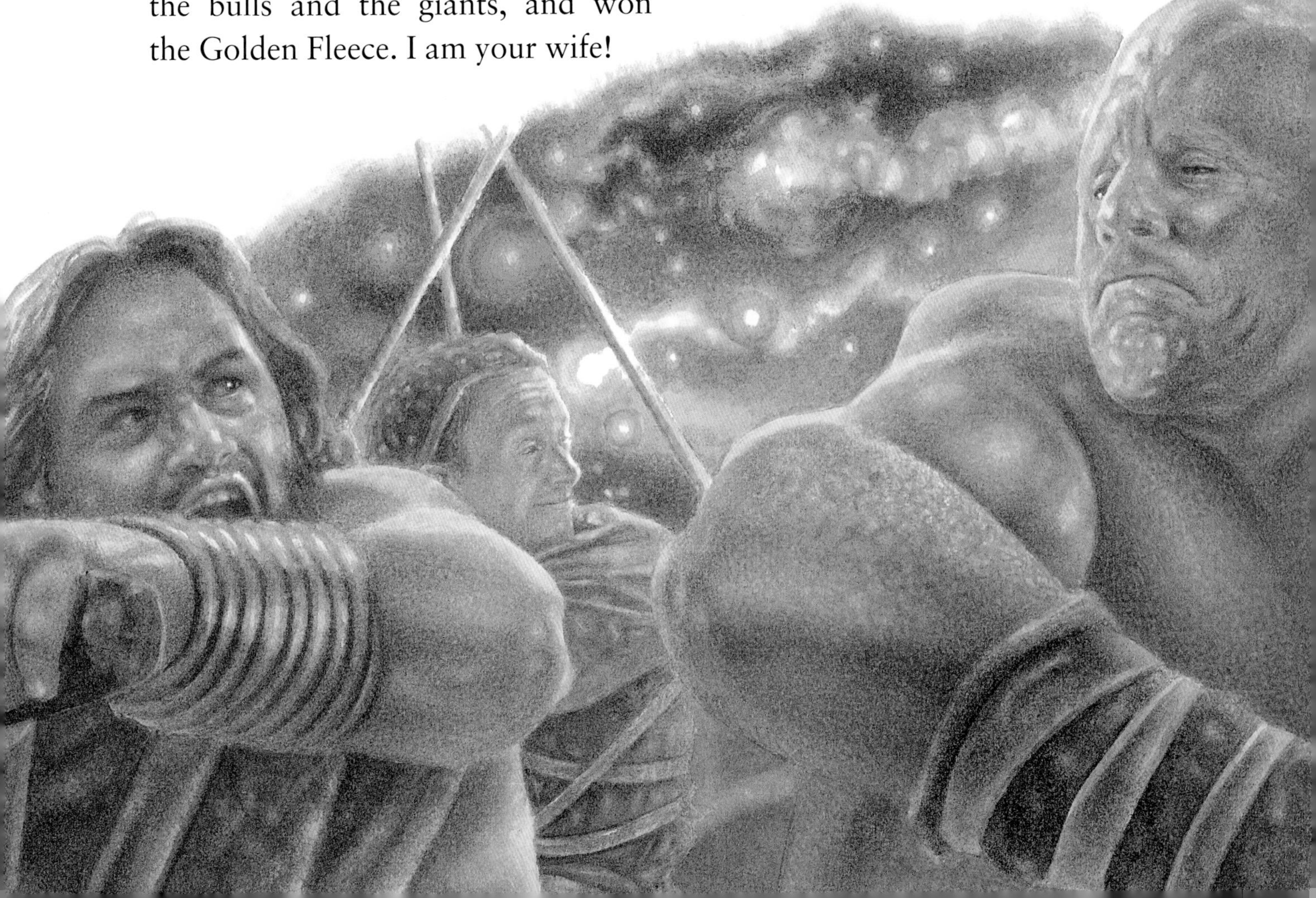

I would rather you slit my throat than abandon me to such a cruel fate!"

Jason did his best to calm her fears.

"Medea, we must avoid a fight at all costs – there are so few of us that we would surely be defeated. Then you would be taken captive, while we would certainly meet a horrible end. But my plan may work. Try to lure your brother to a meeting and I will do the rest."

Reluctantly, Medea agreed. They decided that she would arrange a meeting with Apsyrtos, on the pretext of handing over the Golden Fleece and the Argonauts.

Medea set off for the rendezvous, taking rich gifts, among them Hypsipyle's sacred purple robe made by the three Graces. She met her half-brother that night in the temple of Artemis, and told him that Jason had carried her off by force.

All the while, Jason lay in wait. At a signal from Medea, he leapt out and struck down Apsyrtos, like a butcher axing a bull. Medea quickly turned away, but as the blood gushed from Apsyrtos' fatal wound, it splashed crimson spots all over her silver veil and white robe.

The foul deed done, Jason and Medea hurried to the ship and the crew rowed hard to make their escape. But first they had to deal with the Colchian ship that barred their way. Like a hawk pouncing on a dove, they swept down on its crew and slaughtered every man on board, clearing a route down the estuary.

With Apsyrtos dead and Hera's lightning blinding their path, the Colchian ships soon gave up the chase.

So the *Argo* escaped to the open sea.

Poseidon's Wrath

But the Argonauts could not escape the wrath of Poseidon. Enraged at Jason's bloody deed, he decreed that the Argonauts would suffer for it. So he stirred up the seas, sending shrieking gales and thick black fog to envelop the ship. For a time the crew had to carry the *Argo* overland, before rowing up the Danube to the western shore.

Once back on the high seas, they came to the Siren Rocks, greatly feared by sailors. For lovely mermaids charmed men so sweetly with their song that many dived overboard and drowned. But Orpheus took his lyre and sang so loudly that he drowned out the Siren song.

So the ship sailed on, round the toe of Italy, past needle-sharp cliffs where the dangerous Scylla and Charybdis lay in wait, past the water meadows where Helios the Sun God pastured his white cattle. A savage storm drove the men across the Mediterranean to Libya's desert shore. Once more the crew had to drag their shipwrecked vessel overland.

It was a long time before the stains of Apsyrtos' blood were washed from the ill-starred ship.

Eventually, strong winds blew the *Argo* northwards to Crete. By now, the crew were desperate for water. But the island of Crete was guarded by the Titan Talos, and when he spied the approaching *Argo*, he waded into the sea, hurling rocks, and would not let the heroes land.

Nothing, it seemed, could harm this fearsome sentinel, for he was made of brass.

But Talos had a weak spot. One of his heels contained a pin which sealed in his blood. And once more Medea came to their aid. While she charmed Talos to sleep, little Poias shot an arrow to try to dislodge the pin from the Titan's heel. The arrow hit its mark: Talos' life-blood poured into the sea and, with a deafening crash, he fell down dead upon the shore.

Much relieved, the Argonauts ran to fill their gourds in the island's springs, and headed for home.

Return *of the* Argo

Friends barely recognised the Argonauts as they sailed into the port of Iolcos. The years had taken their toll on the high-spirited band. The handful who returned were older, careworn men.

As for King Pelias, he did not know the weather-beaten figure who walked into his court – until Jason threw down the Golden Fleece.

Pelias turned pale. Then his face grew dark.

"Be gone," he said with a scowl, "before I kill you all!"

Jason's long quest, it seemed, had been in vain. He strode angrily from the palace, brooding on bloody revenge.

But Medea had another idea. "Leave the king to me," she said. "When you see a torch burning on the palace roof, you will know that he is dead."

There was a full moon that night. Wearing her priestess's robe and carrying a leather pouch, Medea went alone to the evil king.

"Sire," she said sweetly, "I am priestess to the goddess Hecate. I have the power to transform old age to youth."

Pelias, who was by now an old and feeble man, wanted nothing more than to regain his lost youth. But he was suspicious. "Prove you can make me young again," he said.

Turning to the king's three daughters, Medea ordered them to prepare a cauldron of boiling water. When it was ready, Medea asked

for an old ram to be brought. This she dropped into the pot with some magic herbs, and put on the lid. To their astonishment, as she removed the lid, a frisky lamb hopped out and ran off bleating!

Pelias was convinced. He lay down on a couch and let Medea charm him to sleep. Then she handed a knife to each of the three princesses.

"To make your father young," she said, "you must cut him into pieces and boil his flesh in the pot of magic herbs."

While the women were about their awful task, Medea sprinkled simple herbs into the pot instead of magical plants. When the water was boiling, she said, "Drop your father's pieces into the pot and stir the mixture well. Now be patient while I go and pray to the full moon."

With that, she hurried to the rooftop and lit a fire. That was the signal: at once, Jason and the heroes ran into the palace – to find Pelias well and truly dead.

So Jason took his rightful place on the throne.

One by one, the heroes went their separate ways, eager to see their homes and loved ones after all their years away.

As for Jason, he soon tired of the city that had brought him so much pain; and he lost all desire for a kingdom gained by the black arts. So he handed over his throne to Pelias' son Acastus who had sailed with him to Colchis.

Yet happiness still eluded him.

The DEATH *of* JASON

As the years passed, Jason grew restless. After his adventures and long years at sea, he found city life irksome and he missed his old friends.

Then Medea fell ill and died. Some say the goddess Hecate made her immortal, and bore her away to the Elysian Fields where she became the goddess of rebirth. There, in her cauldron, she continues to boil those worthy souls who will be born again into another life.

Now there was nothing left to keep Jason in Iolcos. He took a ship and voyaged down the coast to Corinth. There he hung the Golden Fleece in the temple of Zeus, where it rightfully belonged.

After that, Jason wandered through many lands before finally returning to Iolcos.

One day, he made his way down to the shore where the *Argo*'s hulk lay rotting. He sat in the shadow of Hera's prow and recalled the glorious times of old.

In his mind's eye, he saw his old tutor, the centaur Chiron, who reminded him of his youth up in the hills of Mount Pelion. Hera, in her dazzling white robes, smiled down at him. He remembered the building of the *Argo* and the comradeship of its crew – mighty Hercules, bold Pollux and Castor, brave Atalanta and dear Hylas. Brightest of all, he recalled his first sight of the Golden Fleece, and it seemed to shine into his very soul. For a moment he was happy again.

Then, without warning, the heavy prow collapsed and crashed down, crushing him to death. It was as if Hera had taken pity on him and brought him peace.

Yet that is not quite the end of the story. For Zeus, watching from the cloud-capped peak of Mount Olympus, reached down and lifted up the *Argo*'s stern, setting it among the stars for all the world to see. There it joined Aries the Ram, the twins Castor and Pollux, and mighty Hercules. They will forever remind us of Jason and the Argonauts, who braved perils beyond imagination to bring the Golden Fleece back home to Greece.

Sources

Robert Graves, *Greek Myths* (Cassell, London, 1958)
A.R. Hope Moncrieff, *Classical Mythology* (Harrap, London, 1907)
Thomas Bulfinch, *The Golden Age of Myth and Legend* (Wordsworth Editions, Ware, 1993; first published 1855)
Kenneth McLeish, *Children of the Gods* (Longman, Harlow, 1983)
James Reeves, *Heroes and Monsters: Legends of Ancient Greece* (Pan Macmillan, 1962)
Roy Willis (ed.), *World Mythology* (BCA, London, 1993)
Roger Lancelyn Green, *Tales of the Greek Heroes* (Puffin Books, Harmondsworth, 1958)
Michael Gibson, *Gods, Men and Monsters from the Greek Myths* (Eurobook, Glasgow, 1977)
Pamela Oldfield, *Stories from Ancient Greece* (Kingfisher, London, 1988)
Henry Treece, *Jason* (Bodley Head, 1961)

Ancient sources

Apollonius' *The Argonauts* (3rd century B.C.) tells the story of Jason's quest for the Golden Fleece; the same story is told from a modern viewpoint in Robert Graves's novel *The Golden Fleece* (Cassell, London, 1944).
Euripides' play *Medea* (5th century B.C.) describes Medea's vengeance in Corinth when Jason deserts her to marry Glauce.

River Danube

GREECE

Salmydessos

THRACE

ITALY

Sea

Marma

Kyzikos

Hellespont

Lemnos

Mount Pelion

Iolcos

CRETE

ROUTE TAKEN BY THE *ARGO* FROM IOLCOS TO COLCHIS

Black Sea

COLCHIS

ymplegades

Bosphorus

Isle of Ares

Isle of Bebryces

ASIA MINOR

Mediterranean Sea

OTHER CLASSIC PICTURE BOOKS FROM FRANCES LINCOLN

Black Ships Before Troy

Rosemary Sutcliff

Illustrated by Alan Lee

In this fabulous retelling of *The Iliad* Rosemary Sutcliff charts the history of the Trojan War from its origins with Aphrodite and the golden apple, through Paris's abduction of Helen and the heroics of Hector, Ajax and Achilles. Finally, Odysseus conceives a plan to bring the bitter siege to its fiery conclusion.

ISBN 0-7112-1522-7 UK
ISBN 1-84507-359-2 USA

The Wanderings of Odysseus

Rosemary Sutcliff

Illustrated by Alan Lee

Rosemary Sutcliff transforms *The Odyssey* into an enthralling traveller's tale with a spectacular cast of men, magicians and monsters. Alan Lee evokes the golden age of mythical Greece in his portrayal of the greatest voyage of all time.

ISBN 0-7112-1846-3 UK
ISBN 1-84507-360-6 USA

In Search of a Homeland

Penelope Lively

Illustrated by Ian Andrew

The Roman poet Virgil, inspired by the poetry of Homer, wrote his epic *The Aeneid* towards the end of his life. Over two thousand years later, Penelope Lively retells Aeneas's story with pace, poignancy and drama, while Ian Andrew's illustrations bring the characters hauntingly to life.

ISBN 0-7112-1728-9